The Gunpowder Plot
A Time for Treason

Ann Turnbull

Illustrated by Akbar Ali

A & C BLACK
AN IMPRINT OF BLOOMSBURY
LONDON NEW DELHI NEW YORK SYDNEY

For my black cat, Harley

First published 2014 by A & C Black
an imprint of Bloomsbury Publishing Plc
50 Bedford Square, London WC1B 3DP

www.bloomsbury.com

ISBN 978-1-4729-0847-6

A CIP catalogue for this book is available from the British Library.

Printed by CPI Group (UK) Ltd, Croydon CR0 4YY

1 3 5 7 9 10 8 6 4 2

Contents

1

A Letter for Eliza

"Nothing ever happens in London," sighed Eliza.

She put down her needlework and looked out of the window at the wet, wind-shaken garden, where yellow leaves were swirling.

"You're missing your cousin, aren't you?" her governess, Mistress Perks, said. She frowned at Eliza's crossed threads. "Unpick that and do it again."

Eliza began pulling out stitches. She thought of Warwickshire, where her cousin Lucy lived, and where Eliza and her family had been visiting only a few months ago, in the summer. Eliza lived in a town house in Westminster, next to the House of Lords, but Lucy's home was a big country house that had its own deer park.

"I loved seeing the hunters ride out," Eliza said. "And having dancing lessons with Lucy. Oh, and meeting the Lady Elizabeth!"

To their great excitement, the girls had been presented to King James's daughter, Princess Elizabeth, who lived at Coombe Abbey, near Coventry. The princess was only nine years old, like Eliza and Lucy, yet she lived with her own household, far away from her parents and family.

Thinking about this now, Eliza asked, "Why do the royal children not live with the King and Queen?"

"Because of their rank," said Mistress Perks, "and for their safety – and the safety of the realm."

The safety of the realm. That sounded important. Eliza was about to ask more, but from somewhere in the house she heard a door opening, and voices – one of them her father's. A moment later her father came into the room. He was holding a letter, and Eliza immediately recognised the deer's head on its wax seal and knew it was from his cousin – Lucy's father.

Mistress Perks and Eliza both rose and curtseyed.

"Forgive this interruption, Mistress Perks," Eliza's father said, with a smile, "but I have a letter for Eliza, and I know she will be eager to see it."

From inside his own letter he drew another, and handed it to his daughter. It was a single folded sheet of paper, sealed with a blob of wax and marked, '*For Eliza Fenton. Most secret.*'

"Oh!" exclaimed Eliza. "From Lucy!"

Her father left, and Eliza looked beseechingly at her governess. She longed to be alone to open the letter, but could not leave the room without permission.

Mistress Perks gave in. "You may go to your chamber now, Eliza."

Eliza hurried upstairs. In the small chilly bedchamber she broke the seal and opened the piece of paper.

It was blank.

Eliza smiled. She went to the fireplace and blew on the embers of last night's fire until little flames sprang up and began to give off heat. She held the letter above the fire. Would it be hot enough? Yes!

Reddish-yellow marks appeared on the paper. As the heat increased she began to see words. It was another of Lucy's secret letters, written in orange juice, and dated 26th October 1605.

'*Sweet cousin,*' wrote Lucy, '*Our enemies are everywhere. Burn this after reading it.*' Lucy always said that. Sometimes the two of them wrote in secret code, but they liked invisible ink better. '*My father is to attend the State Opening of Parliament in London on the fifth of November,*' Lucy continued, '*and the good news is that he will bring me with him, to your house. Mother has gone to Leicester to see Aunt Warren, who has been ill. I did fear someone had poisoned my aunt, but Mother says no, it is only her bad knee.*' The next words were paler as the orange juice ran out: '*...must watch for danger at every...trust no one...*' And then there was a faint signature: '*Lucy Fenton*'.

All Eliza's boredom vanished in a moment. The fifth of November was less than a week away. Perhaps Lucy and her father had already left Warwickshire. They could be here any day.

Lucy will share my room, Eliza thought. *It will be such fun!*

Black Cat and Coal Dust

"Sir Stephen Chelwall and his wife were caught with two priests hidden in their house," whispered Lucy, as the girls lay in bed on the evening of Lucy's arrival. "The priests were in a secret space under the floorboards."

Eliza's eyes widened. "How do you know?"

"I heard Father and Mother talking."

Eliza felt scared, yet excited. Her family was careful never to speak of such things. Her father was a courtier – always ready at any time to attend upon the King – and both her parents regularly went to church and called themselves Protestants. But now that she was older Eliza understood that they, like Lucy's parents, were Catholics at heart. And that was dangerous. It was not against the law to be a Catholic, but hearing Catholic mass was forbidden, and there were heavy fines for hiding priests.

"The priests will be executed," whispered Lucy. They both knew this would be done in the most horrible way.

"We must not talk about it," said Eliza, with a shudder.

And they said no more. They blew out the candle and went to sleep.

But next morning, as soon as their lessons with Mistress Perks were over, they began their favourite game of spies – just as they had when Eliza visited Lucy's home. Lucy had confided in Eliza that it was her ambition to be a spy. "Ladies are excellent at watching and reporting," she said. "My mother says so."

They could not go out. The wind flung great drops of rain against the windows and the cobbles outside were shining wet. Instead, Lucy took out a little notebook from the pocket under her gown and passed it to Eliza. "We must make a list of all the people in the house," she said. "Anyone could be an enemy."

Eliza wrote down all the names, from her parents, her governess and the maids and manservant, down to the kitchen folk:

'Mistress Rowley, cook.

Walter Bennett, handyman.

Anne and Bessy, kitchen maids.

Mouser, cat.'

"I don't think any of those are enemies," she said, "though Mistress Rowley says Mouser is not living up to his name and keeps disappearing."

Eliza saw a spark of interest brighten her cousin's face.

"I wonder where he goes?" said Lucy. And she wrote down:

'Mouser – suspect.'

"Can we meet him?" she asked.

"Yes," said Eliza. "And if we go now, Mistress Rowley might give us sweetmeats. I can smell baking."

They hurried downstairs, taking their notes with them. The kitchen was a busy place, the fire hot, the table laden with pastry and stuffings and chopped meat, the maidservants scurrying around – all in honour of the visitors.

Mistress Rowley, her face rosy from the fire, curtseyed as she brushed floury hands on her apron.

"What a clever pair you are, with all your reading and writing!" she said, glancing at the notebook in Lucy's hand. "But I expect you'd like a cinnamon bun each – same as any other little girls?"

"Yes, please!"

She handed them one each, and the girls were quiet as they enjoyed the warm, crumbly buns.

The black cat, Mouser, sidled into the kitchen.

"Now, where have you been, Mouser?"

demanded Mistress Rowley. “Look at the cobwebs on his whiskers! He’s been on the prowl somewhere.”

The girls knelt to stroke him.

“He’s all dirty!” exclaimed Eliza, giggling. “My hand is black!”

"So is mine."

Lucy got up and moved towards the corner that Mouser had emerged from – but Mistress Rowley stood in her way.

"No you don't, young mistress – not in your silk gown and pretty slippers! That doorway leads to the storeroom and the coal hole."

Lucy stepped back, and Eliza saw her examining her hands.

"Coal dust," said Lucy.

"At least we *have* a coal store now, and don't have to rent it," Mistress Rowley said, turning back to her pastry-making. "There's Mistress Bright across the way complaining that she's lost hers since Master Whynniard let the big cellar to some gentleman or other. Though why any gentleman would need a cellar that size all to himself, goodness knows. Goes all the way under the House of Lords, that one does. There's a door in our storeroom that used to connect to it. Well, now, young mistresses, I have work to do."

She shooed them out.

Eliza and Lucy were not much interested in who rented the big cellar or where the entrances were – though back upstairs they made notes, as any good spy would. But then Eliza looked out of the window and said, "It's stopped raining. We can go out this afternoon."

3

A Stranger

"I must make a visit to the haberdasher's and buy some sewing silks," said Mistress Perks. "You girls can accompany me."

Eliza wished she and Lucy could go out alone, but that would never be allowed. As young gentlewomen they were always accompanied and supervised.

The governess led them out through the cloisters to the open area of shops and market stalls. Here, all was noise and bustle. They saw squawking chickens hung up by their feet, a dairymaid leading a cow, women selling bread and fragrant herbs, an apothecary's shop, and a milliner's.

Eliza watched her cousin looking about, interested in everything.

"There are so many little shops!" Lucy exclaimed. "You are lucky to have them so close to home, Eliza."

Some of the shops and houses were tiny, squeezed into corners. All the old buildings seemed to be joined at some point, with floors on different levels, and extra rooms and windows added bit by bit over hundreds of years.

"That hall up there is called the Prince's Chamber," Eliza told her cousin. "Father says they use it as a robing room for the Lords when they assemble."

Beneath the Prince's Chamber was a row of houses and shops.

As they turned to enter the haberdasher's, a man came out of the house next door. His doublet was dirty, and he wore a battered high-crowned hat with the brim tilted to shade his face, but Eliza noticed his red-brown hair and beard and his bold gaze, and the way he held himself – straight and tall, like a soldier.

He is dressed as a working man, she thought, *and yet he has the bearing of a gentleman.*

The man saw Eliza looking at him and glared at her. He turned away swiftly, disappearing around the corner into Parliament Place.

Mistress Perks drew the girls with her into the shop.

As the governess hesitated over different coloured threads, Eliza whispered to Lucy, "Did you see that man?"

"Yes. Do you know him?"

Eliza shook her head.

"He looks like an enemy," said Lucy.

* * *

"I can tell you who that is," said Walter Bennett.

The girls had gone down to the kitchen in the hope of discovering more and had found

Walter the handyman there, fixing a broken window catch.

"His name's John Johnson," Walter said, "and he's a servant of Sir Thomas Percy that lives in Gray's Inn Road. Johnson's the new tenant at Master Whynniard's house – moved there in the spring, so I heard."

Eliza looked at Lucy who frowned, and riffled through the notes they had made after listening to Mistress Rowley. "Sir Thomas Percy? Is he the gentleman who is renting the big cellar?"

Walter Bennett looked at her in surprise. "Yes, that'll be him! Seems you know as much as I do, almost. I heard this John

Johnson is guarding a stock of fuel there for the gentleman. I saw him moving some firewood in a while ago."

"Doesn't Sir Thomas Percy have his own cellar at Gray's Inn Road?" asked Lucy.

"I don't know, mistress. You don't ask questions of gentry, do you?"

"*I* do," said Lucy. "But then my father is a lord."

"Of course," said the handyman, giving a little bow.

"Oh!" exclaimed Eliza. "Here comes Mouser!" She knelt to stroke the cat. "He's all dusty again."

As they went back upstairs, Lucy said,

"We need to follow that cat. And John Johnson. They could be in league together."

Eliza smiled. *I like this game*, she thought. And she remarked, "It will be difficult to get out on our own."

Lucy agreed. "But my mother says that a lady can always find a way to do what she wants."

4 Following John Johnson

They found a way the next morning, after church. All the time, while the congregation was gathering for the service, Eliza and Lucy whispered, twisting and turning to see who was coming in, till Eliza's mother slapped her daughter's hand and hissed, "Sit still and be quiet! You shame me!"

Eliza tried to obey. But then Lucy nudged her. "*He's* here!" And Eliza risked a glance around the edge of the pew and saw the tall stranger, John Johnson, slipping into a seat at the back of the church. He took off his hat and lowered his head as if in silent prayer, but Eliza still felt sure that he was playing a part and was not what he seemed. *Perhaps he is privately a Catholic*, she thought, *like my father*. But there was something fierce and secretive about John Johnson that was not like her father at all. She pulled back quickly and lowered her own eyes.

When the service was over Eliza saw

John Johnson leave the church ahead of most of the congregation.

"Watch where he goes!" whispered Lucy.

"I am!" Eliza tried to keep an eye on Johnson's hat as he moved away through the crowd of people. She wanted to hurry after him – but, to her annoyance, the adults paused in the churchyard to talk. Eliza's mother said she wished to go straight home, but the two men decided they would walk for a while.

Eliza and Lucy hopped about impatiently. They had lost John Johnson now.

"Father..." began Lucy.

And her father said, "Shall we take the girls?"

"That would be a kindness, cousin. Thank you," said Eliza's mother.

And to Eliza she whispered, "Now, be good, and behave like a lady. Let us hope the fresh air blows that unbecoming fidgetiness out of you."

Then Eliza's mother and her servants turned back towards home, and Eliza and Lucy were left with their fathers.

The gentlemen led the way, strolling through the streets and down towards the river. They wanted to talk, and took little notice of the girls, who skipped along beside them, feeling the breeze on their faces and gazing out at all the boats coming and going on the river.

Their fathers spoke of the King's return to London from a hunting expedition, and of the State Opening of Parliament which they would attend in two days' time.

We'll be able to watch the procession and see the King arrive, thought Eliza.

"Eliza!" whispered Lucy, catching her arm. "Look!"

John Johnson had reappeared. He had hailed one of the boats that ferried people to and fro across the river from Parliament Stairs to Lambeth. He was now on board, standing up straight and steady in the boat without a hint of a wobble as it moved out into the current.

So he was going to Lambeth. And the same thought came to both of them.

"If he's away..."

"We could look around near that house he's renting..."

But there was no chance to do so immediately, so they enjoyed scurrying along the muddy paths until they were pink-cheeked and untidy and the hems of their gowns were splashed with dirt.

* * *

"You are a pair of hoydens!" Eliza's mother complained when they returned.

"Go and find Cecily. She'll comb your hair and re-pin it. Then you may both come and sew with me and read the Bible."

But Eliza and Lucy wanted to go out before John Johnson came back across the river. And Cecily, Eliza's nursemaid, was nowhere to be seen.

"Let's go now," said Eliza, surprising herself with her own daring. "If we're quick, they won't know."

It took only moments to sneak out into the Sunday quiet of Westminster and make their way to the little house on the corner of Parliament Place.

Eliza felt both excited and frightened.

Was this still a game of spies, she wondered, like the games they had played at Lucy's home in Warwickshire? Mouser the cat had secrets, as cats do, and it would be fun to discover them. But John Johnson was different. There was something not right about him. Eliza felt sure he was in disguise, and that their game was on the brink of becoming real.

The door of the house was shut.

"It'll be locked," said Lucy. "Let's look through the window."

They peered in. But they could see little through the small greenish panes.

"There's a chair. And a table with a candlestick on it," said Eliza.

"No weapons. No documents." Lucy looked disappointed. "Where is the cellar – the big cellar where Walter Bennett said John Johnson was guarding the firewood?"

"It's under the House of Lords. But you can't see it from here," said Eliza. "There are buildings all around it."

"Where do these steps go?" asked Lucy.

Eliza looked at the short flight of steps that led down between the house and the next-door shop. "I don't know."

"Let's go and see," Lucy said.

Eliza didn't want to. What if someone saw them and told her mother? What if John Johnson came back and caught them?

But Lucy was already on her way down. Her voice echoed as she called, "There's a courtyard..."

Reluctantly, Eliza followed.

At the bottom was a wall, but the passage twisted to the left and opened out into a small courtyard – a dank, dark place between tall buildings, with moss growing on the walls and bird droppings everywhere. Eliza looked up and saw a small square of sky. She felt trapped.

"Let's go back," she whispered.

Lucy wasn't listening. "The passage goes on. And there's a building that goes all the way along it." She turned to Eliza. "Could that be the cellar?"

Before Eliza could look, or think, they heard heavy footsteps coming down the stairs.

"It's him!"

"Hide!"

They looked around frantically.

"Over there!"

A water butt stood in one corner of the courtyard. They dived behind it, pulling in the layers and flounces of their skirts, and squeezed close together, just as the person came into view.

It was a woman – a servant – carrying a great basket of linen. Eliza felt weak with relief. But she held her breath and kept still as the

woman plodded past and disappeared around the corner into the long passage, her footsteps gradually growing fainter.

At last the girls crept out.

“I thought – ”

“I was so scared – ”

Now that their fright was over they began to giggle.

"Your gown! It's got green moss stains on it."

"Yours has got something worse."

"Ugh! Let's go home!"

Still giggling, they ran up the stairs. And Eliza, leading the way, stepped onto the pavement and ran straight into John Johnson.

5

A Knock at the Door

"Oh!" Eliza cried out.

She felt as if her knees would give way. Behind her, Lucy gave a little shriek.

John Johnson and Eliza stared at each other. For an instant his look was fierce and pitiless, like that of the hawk she'd seen last summer on a hunter's wrist in Warwickshire.

Then he changed. He hunched his shoulders, took off his hat and held it in front of him as he bowed and muttered,

"Your pardon, mistress."

He had the look of a servant as he shuffled aside to let them pass.

But I saw his real face, thought Eliza. *John Johnson is no servant. He is playing a part, I'm sure of it. He is dangerous. And he knows we are following him.*

She seized Lucy's hand, and the two of them ran off down the street as fast as they could. They didn't look back, but Eliza could feel John Johnson watching them till they turned the corner.

* * *

"Where *have* the gentlemen taken you?" cried Cecily, as she surveyed the two dishevelled girls. "Mud, cobwebs – and what are these nasty green stains?"

She unlaced their gowns and made them change into clean clothes, then set about untangling their hair.

"Ow!" wailed Eliza.

"It's for your own good, Mistress Eliza. Your mother mustn't see you like this. She's already cross, waiting for you. Where have you been?"

"Nowhere much," said Eliza. "Ouch!"

Later, on their way downstairs, Lucy whispered, "We must meet and talk privately."

But Eliza's mother kept them both under her eye for the rest of the day, reading from the Bible and working on their embroidery. Eliza thought they would have to wait until bedtime, but in the evening, when they were all finishing supper, there came a loud knock at the main door.

Eliza heard her father's manservant talking to someone. Then he came in and spoke quietly to her father and uncle, who both got up at once and went out into the hall.

In the dining room, all the clatter of plates and spoons stopped, and Eliza knew her mother was listening intently. So were Eliza and Lucy.

There were several men's voices on the other side of the door. They sounded urgent and serious. Eliza caught the words "warning…", "a letter…", "the King's person…"

Then the visitors' voices rose as they moved towards the door: "If you see or hear anything unusual…"

"We will, most certainly," her father said.

Eliza and Lucy looked at each other. Eliza knew they were both thinking the same thing.

"Mother," she said, "Lucy and I have noticed something unusual."

"Oh!" Her mother seemed to see the girls for the first time. "Eliza, how many times have I told you not to listen to private conversations? Go upstairs to your bedchamber now, both of you."

"But, Mother... There is a man – there is something strange about him..."

But her mother took no notice. Eliza knew she thought this was just one of their games. And she also knew that her mother was alarmed by what the gentlemen had been saying.

Upstairs in their bedchamber, Eliza and Lucy talked in whispers about what they had just heard.

"I'm sure it means danger to the King," said Lucy. "We ought to inform our fathers of our suspicions."

Lucy had a way of making things sound important. Eliza knew she must go down again and speak to her father, even if he was angry.

They found their fathers deep in discussion. It was not a good time, and the gentlemen were not pleased to see them – but Lucy's father gave her permission to speak. "Father," she said, "we have been watching someone we believe is an enemy."

Eliza remembered something Mistress Perks had said, and added, "We think this concerns the safety of the realm."

The men exchanged a glance, and Lucy's father sighed. "Lucy," he said, "we have no time for your games now. I am displeased at this interruption. Please leave us."

"You too, Eliza," said her father sternly.

"It's not a game – " Eliza began. But her father's look silenced her.

The two of them retreated once again to their bedchamber.

"What can we *do*?" asked Eliza.

They sat on the bed, and Lucy took out her notebook and read through everything she had written down.

"Mouser..." she said at last.

"*Mouser?*"

"Mouser goes exploring in the coal store... And John Johnson is storing fuel in the big cellar under the House of Lords... And – do you remember? – Mistress Rowley said there used to be a way into that big cellar from this house..."

Eliza understood – and felt excited. "So, if we follow Mouser, we might find the way in?"

On Mouser's Trail

They waited till night – when everyone had gone to bed, even Mistress Rowley and the maids.

"The servants work late," said Eliza, "and Bessy – she's the youngest maid – she sleeps in the kitchen."

They listened to the household sounds: doors closing, footsteps on the stairs, murmured "goodnights" from the family.

Outside, in the street, the watchman

passed by with his lantern. "Ten o'clock, and all's well!" he called.

Still they waited, dressed in their nightgowns, and sitting up straight so as not to fall asleep.

At last the house fell silent except for creaking timbers and the scuttering of mice in the wainscot.

"Let's go," whispered Eliza.

They crept downstairs.

The kitchen was dark, and they paused in the doorway until their eyes became accustomed to the gloom. The fire was banked up, and in front of it Bessy lay asleep on a pallet. They tiptoed past her.

Eliza gasped as she felt the brush of a furry body on her legs and heard a faint "prrrow..."

Mouser trotted towards the open storeroom doorway.

"Quick!" whispered Lucy.

They followed the cat into the storeroom as he padded past shelves laden with cleaning materials and tools. Further in Eliza could see the coal store and, next to it, bundles of firewood piled up and stacked against the wall. Mouser disappeared behind the stack.

The girls crouched and followed him, crawling on hands and knees. Eliza's sleeve caught on a nail and she felt it tear.

Now I'll be in more trouble, she thought.

"Look!" Lucy's voice was full of suppressed excitement.

Eliza peered, and saw a door. There was a big hole in it near the base, where the wood had rotted – and disappearing through the hole was Mouser's tail.

"It must be the door to the big cellar," said Lucy. "The one Mistress Rowley said hadn't been used for years."

They tried the handle. "It's locked," said Eliza.

She knelt and pushed her head and shoulders through the hole.

"What can you see?" asked Lucy.

"Nothing. I can feel a stone floor – oh, and walls. It's a passage!"

She came back out, and they looked at each other. Eliza wondered if Lucy felt as scared as she did. She took a breath. "Shall we go in?"

They crawled through – Eliza first, then Lucy – and stood up. The stone floor of the passage sent a chill up through their silk slippers and they shivered in the cold air. Eliza felt for Lucy's hand as they moved forward.

To their relief, the passage was short. Almost at once they became aware of a faint greyish light and reached another door.

There was no sound from Mouser, and they could not see him. He must have found a way in.

"He went underneath," Eliza whispered. "Look! The whole bottom of the door has rotted away. But the gap's too small for us."

She wrenched at the damp, crumbly wood, and a big piece broke off, startling her.

Both girls froze. What if someone was there, on the other side, watching?

But Eliza heard nothing. Cautiously they enlarged the gap some more, and then Lucy, who was thinner than Eliza, began to squeeze herself through.

Eliza breathed in, and followed.

The other side of the door was blocked with heaps of wooden crates and boxes, scrap timber, and masonry. They began creeping forward, careful not to dislodge anything.

A small "prrp!" alerted them to Mouser, but almost at once he crept away under the debris to some secret place of his own.

Eliza, squirming further in, whispered, “There are barrels here.”

She saw now that they were in what must indeed be the big cellar under the House of Lords. It was huge, with rows of pillars and arched alcoves. Her father had told her it had once been the kitchens of the great hall, back in the olden days.

Some feeble light came from narrow windows high in the walls. It showed great stacks of firewood and coal down both sides of a central space. And behind the fuel, where she and Lucy had come in, were many barrels, stacked in rows.

"It must be wine," Eliza said. "Perhaps it's for the State Opening of Parliament, when the King comes, and all the lords."

She moved forward to squeeze between the piles of firewood – and at the same moment there was the sound of a door opening on the far side of the cellar, and someone else came in, carrying a lantern that lit his face.

Eliza gasped and slid back into the shelter of the woodpile.

"It's him!" she whispered. "John Johnson!"

In the Cellar

Eliza and Lucy hardly dared breathe. They crouched low and hid behind the barrels as John Johnson walked up and down the length of the cellar, looking about him. His lantern cast looming shadows on the walls and ceiling.

Supposing he sees us? thought Eliza. She pressed up against the barrels and peeped between them. The shadow of the man in his tall hat reared over her.

Then a sudden scrabbling and a soft thump set Eliza's heart racing and made the lantern swing wildly in John Johnson's hand.

"Mouser..." breathed Lucy.

Eliza saw the black cat caught in the beam of light, with a mouse dangling from his jaws. He wailed eerily – and for an instant Johnson looked as frightened as Eliza felt. He took a step backwards and crossed himself.

Mouser trotted away – straight towards the girls.

John Johnson followed.

He'll see us! thought Eliza, in terror.

The light from the lantern swung over and around them, and they shrank back into the shadows to hide among the piles of boxes.

Johnson frowned and moved the lantern about. He peered into the darkness.

"Nothing," he muttered at last.

But he seemed disturbed, and they heard him pacing up and down again and saw the light swinging to and fro, making shadows leap along the walls. Then he became still, and Eliza heard only a faint murmuring. "What's he doing?" she whispered.

Lucy could see through a small gap. "He's kneeling down. I think he's praying."

They stayed still for what felt like a long time, not daring to move an inch.

At last Lucy said, "He's getting up."

They heard a door open, the light disappeared, and there was the sound of a key turning in a lock. He was gone.

"Oh!" breathed Eliza and Lucy together.

Slowly, they crawled out, stood up, and held onto each other, trembling.

Now the cellar seemed huge and shadowy around them. Eliza heard creaks and patterings and a rustle of wings. Could it be bats? Or demons? She called softly to Mouser, but he didn't come.

"Let's go back," she said. "I'm scared."

They felt their way back to the door, squeezed under it, and hurried along the passage to Eliza's house. As she crawled

through the hole in the door and then out from behind the woodstack, Eliza thought about what they had seen. What was John Johnson doing in the cellar? Was it something to do with those barrels of wine? She felt sure it was.

The two of them stood up, brushed dust from their clothes, crept into the kitchen, and saw –

A ghost!

Screams rang out. Eliza screamed. Lucy screamed. And the ghost screamed – it was Bessy, in her nightgown.

"Oh, Bessy, hush!" gasped Eliza.

"Oh, Mistress!" Bessy curtseyed and

began to cry. "Oh, I thought you were ghosts!"

"We thought *you* were," said Lucy. "And now – "

Now they were caught. Mistress Rowley appeared in the kitchen in her nightgown and cap, a candle in her hand. At the sight of Lucy and Eliza she too gave a shriek.

"Oh! Whatever – ? Your linen...your hair!"

In the candlelight Eliza saw that her nightgown was torn and dirty. Lucy's was the same, and her hair was full of fragments of wood.

"We have something important to tell – " Lucy began.

But there was no chance to explain.

Voices and footsteps sounded from above; doors opened; and into the kitchen came first Cecily, then Mistress Perks, then Eliza's parents, and finally Lucy's father, all talking and all wearing nightcaps – which made Eliza want to giggle, despite her fear.

Mistress Rowley calmed Bessy, while Eliza's mother exclaimed in horror at the sight of the girls. "You should both be beaten!" she said. "Where *have* you been?"

"In the cellar," said Lucy. "The big cellar under the House of Lords. And we need to tell the gentlemen what we saw."

"You will do no such thing!" cried Eliza's mother. "Not in your nightclothes! It is most immodest! You will go straight up to your bedchamber and – ”

Her husband interrupted her. “My dear, we are all in our nightclothes and anxious to return to bed. But here we are, awake, and it seems the girls have something to tell us.” He glanced at his cousin. “I think we should hear it?” And Lucy’s father nodded.

So, once again, Eliza and Lucy found themselves in a private room, face to face with their fathers.

They tried to describe what had happened.

“You went into the great cellar?” Eliza’s father said. “But that door has been blocked for years. What were you doing down there?”

Lucy explained about John Johnson. "We don't believe he is really a servant. That's a disguise. I think he is a spy – "

"*I* think," said Eliza, "that he's a thief. He's planning to steal the barrels of wine."

Her father looked puzzled. "What barrels of wine?"

"The ones stored there."

"I thought you said there was firewood and coal stored there?"

"There is, and the barrels are behind it – rows and rows of them. Are they for a feast after the State Opening of Parliament? I thought – " But the two men were looking at each other and frowning.

"The Lords have no wine stored in that cellar," said Eliza's father. "You say it's behind the firewood – hidden?"

"Yes," said Eliza and Lucy together.

Eliza's father turned to his cousin. "We must report this immediately."

Lucy's father agreed. "Lucy," he said, "you have not invented this? If you have, I shall be angry."

Lucy was indignant. "No! We both saw the barrels."

"Go up to bed, then," Eliza's father said. "You were right to tell us."

"Will Mother punish us?" Eliza felt tired and tearful now.

"Probably not. But tomorrow you must stay indoors with her."

The girls went upstairs together, almost too weary to talk. Except that Eliza said, "I do hope Mouser is not in danger."

8

A Midnight Raid

There was a strange atmosphere in the house the next day. The girls' parents talked together in low, troubled tones. They sounded shocked and fearful.

Eliza and Lucy longed to know what was going on, but Mistress Perks kept them busy with lessons, and no one would tell them anything.

They were sent to bed early.

Hours later, in the dead of night, Eliza was

woken by voices in the street outside. Then came the sound of tramping boots and the clink of metal.

Soldiers! she thought.

She got up and opened the window.

A group of soldiers was approaching – and they had a prisoner with them.

"Lucy!" she whispered.

But Lucy was already awake and sliding out of bed. She leaned beside Eliza on the windowsill.

"It's John Johnson," she said.

As the group came closer Eliza saw that she was right. Two of the soldiers held lanterns and their light fell on the face of

John Johnson. The man did not struggle. But he must have heard the girls whispering, for suddenly he glanced up at the open window and saw them. Eliza jumped in fright and pulled Lucy down beside her, below the sill. Hidden there, they heard the soldiers move on.

"He will go to the Tower," said Lucy.

"Yes." It gave Eliza a strange feeling to think that their suspicions had led to a man being arrested and taken to prison.

* * *

In the morning a servant summoned Eliza and Lucy to appear before their parents.

All three adults looked serious.

Both girls curtseyed. Eliza felt small and frightened. Lucy's hand crept into hers and she knew her cousin must be feeling the same.

But no one was angry with them.

"We have been asked by the captain of

the guard to thank you for reporting your suspicions of John Johnson," Eliza's father said. "I will tell you what happened because we don't want you hearing rumours or listening to servants' tittle-tattle. There was a midnight raid on the great cellar. The suspect was found there with thirty-six barrels of gunpowder – "

"*Gunpowder!*" exclaimed Eliza and Lucy together.

"Thirty-six barrels of gunpowder, and a fuse."

Eliza and Lucy stared at each other. Those barrels! They'd never thought of gunpowder.

"He has been taken to the Tower for questioning," Eliza's father continued. "It is believed his plan was to blow up the House of Lords this very day when Parliament assembled and His Majesty King James, Queen Anne and Prince Henry and all the lords were there."

"So – you too, Uncle. And my father," said Lucy.

She gazed at her father in such shock that he bent down and hugged her. "Both of us. And possibly all of you in this house as well, for there was a mighty quantity of powder."

"But – why?" exclaimed Eliza.

"Many Catholics are angry because

His Majesty has not granted them the freedom of worship they hoped for," said her father. "The authorities were alerted by letter a few days ago that a great blow would be struck at Westminster today. Now they will question the prisoner to find out who the other plotters are."

* * *

Later that morning, Lucy sat writing busily in her notebook, while Eliza gazed out of the window and thought about what might have happened. She imagined the company assembling in the great hall above the cellar, the Lords robed in silks and furs, King James resplendent in his crown and cloth of gold, and with him Queen Anne and Prince Henry. The bishops would be there, and all the courtiers like her father, and the ushers and trumpeters and standard-bearers.

If the gunpowder had ignited, they would all have been blown to pieces. Perhaps she and Lucy and her mother and all their household would have died too.

Who would do such a thing?

9

Mouser's Secret

'*His name is Guy Fawkes, not John Johnson.*' Lucy was reading aloud to Eliza from her notebook. '*He is a Catholic gentleman from Yorkshire and was a soldier in the service of the King of Spain. They are questioning him in the Tower.*'

That means torture, thought Eliza, with a shudder.

'*The plotters are on the run and trying to raise a rebellion in the Midlands,*' Lucy continued. '*Several plotters have blown themselves up in an accident with their gunpowder. Mistress Perks says this is God's judgment.*'

Lucy and her father had stayed on in London longer than planned because of the emergency. Eliza was glad. She loved having Lucy to stay. And these were interesting times – but also alarming ones.

"Is it true," Eliza asked her mother, "that they planned to capture the Lady Elizabeth from Coombe Abbey and make her their queen – to do whatever they told her?"

"Yes, it's true," her mother said.

"We met her," said Lucy.

It was shocking to think of the princess – a girl of their age – being the prisoner of such men. And they had other worries. The plotters were nearly all Catholic gentlemen from the Midlands, and the girls' parents were acquainted with some of them.

"Are we safe?" Eliza asked. "They are accusing Catholics of treason." She looked searchingly at her mother. "My father is secretly a Catholic, isn't he?"

"Your father is a loyal servant of the King, and you know he attends the Protestant church."

"But..."

"But the old queen, Elizabeth, said she did not want to look into men's hearts. And I think King James is the same." She put her arms around both girls. "You have nothing to fear."

Eliza felt comforted. But another thing had been worrying her.

"There's Mouser..." she began.

"Who is Mouser?" Eliza's mother did not spend much time in the kitchen.

Eliza and Lucy gabbled to explain.

"The kitchen cat – "

"We last saw him in the cellar – "

"But then soldiers came in and cleared it – "

"And we heard they stopped up some of the entrances – "

"We don't know whether Mouser escaped! You told us we must not go into the kitchen again – "

"Enough!" cried Eliza's mother. "You may ask Mistress Rowley about Mouser. Go and ask her now."

* * *

Mistress Rowley was pleased to see them.

"I have news for you young gentlewomen," she said. "Your friend Mouser –"

"Is he safe?" Eliza looked around anxiously. There was no sign of Mouser.

"He's not only safe, he's had kittens!"

"*Kittens!*"

"Come and see," said Mistress Rowley.

There were some shelves near the fireplace with kitchen things stored on them: a pestle and mortar, some jugs and bowls. On the bottom shelf was a basket full of rags. And in the basket was Mouser, curled up and purring, with three – no, four! – kittens.

"Oh!" exclaimed Eliza in delight.

Both girls dropped to their knees beside the basket. The kittens were not at all pretty yet; they were damp, blind and scrabbling. But their tiny mewing made Eliza and Lucy love them already.

"None of us noticed," confessed Mistress Rowley. "Looking back, I remember he was a bit fat, and extra hungry – "

"She," said Lucy.

"She – yes. And she kept disappearing. Down that cellar, hunting, I suppose, or looking for somewhere to make a nest."

"Will you keep the kittens?" asked Eliza.

"Well, I'd like a couple more cats, to keep the mice down. But the other two... Walter will drown them, I expect."

"Oh, no!" Eliza and Lucy protested together. And Eliza said, "I could take one – for a pet – if Mother will let me."

"And I want one, too!" said Lucy.

"But you're going home soon, aren't you, Mistress Lucy? They won't be weaned for several weeks."

"Then *I'll* take both," said Eliza. "One for me and one for Lucy, when she visits. I'm sure my mother will say yes."

* * *

Eliza dipped her quill pen in the freshly squeezed orange juice she had begged from Mistress Rowley, and wrote:

'8th January, 1606.

Dear cousin Lucy,

Secret news!

At last the kittens are weaned and I have ours with me. I wish you could see them. They interrupt my lessons and make me laugh. I have drawn you a picture of them – in ink, because they are both black. Yours is a girl and has a white bib and two white feet, and mine is a boy and has a white tip to his tail.

Many more gunpowder plotters have been

arrested. Mistress Perks says they will all be executed.

My kitten is called Midnight. What will you call yours? Write soon and tell me.

Your loving cousin,

Eliza Fenton.'

Plague: A Cross on the Door
Ann Turnbull

In the long, hot summer of 1665, the plague comes to London. Sam is a servant boy with no family of his own. When his master dies, Sam is left alone, a prisoner in an empty building with a cross on the door to mark it as a plague house.

The first of Sam's adventures. Can he escape? And even if he does, will he be able to survive on London's ravaged streets?

£4.99 ISBN 9781408186879

The Great Fire: A city in Flames
Ann Turnbull

"In sixteen hundred and sixty-six,
London burned like rotten sticks."

Left alone and homeless by the Great Plague, Sam struggled to survive. He was lucky to get a job working for the Giraud family. Though Andre, the son of his boss, doesn't make life easy.

And then a fire breaks out on Pudding Lane. Before anyone fully realises what's happening, London's burning ... and this fire can't be put out. Now it's time for Sam to prove what he's really worth. If he can get out alive...

£5.99 ISBN 9781408186862

The Gunpowder Plot Unclassified: Secrets Revealed!
Nick Hunter

The Gunpowder Plot could have potentially destroyed the House of Lords, taking with it countless lives, including that of King James I of England. How was this great tragedy prevented?

From Robert Catesby to Guy Fawkes and exactly how this plot was uncovered, *The Gunpowder Plot Unclassified* takes readers on a journey back in time to discover the plans behind this incredible part of history and how they were prevented just in time.

£10.99 ISBN 9781472908568